THE TALE AND ITS MASTER

Michael Rutherford

THE TALE
AND ITS MASTER

SPRING HARBOR PRESS

Published by Spring Harbor Press in 1986
Spring Harbor Press is a Division of Spring Harbor, Ltd.
Box 346, Delmar, New York 12054

Single copies may be ordered from the publisher.
Spring Harbor Press pays the postage.
New York State residents add sales tax.

Our dragon cover and initial letters were designed
by Ed Atkeson of Berg Design.

To John P. MacArthur

NCE UPON A TIME, IN the small town of Smunsk, during the reign of Cinnabar the Second, a baby was born into the Guild of Seers, Speakers, Dreamers, Storytellers, and Non-Fanatical Prophets. As the midwife drew the caul from the infant's head, the wind rose and shook the small house like the beating of great wings. The night itself seemed dissolved in the dark rain that flooded the streets. The old woman tied the cord, snipped it with rune-etched scissors, and passed the child to its grateful, weary mother. His loud cries and florid face augured well for his future.

On the tenth day of life, Simon the fat Guildmaster came and crumbled the eggshell of an evening thrush over the boy's lips, so he would sing with limpid clarity. Then with a feather dipped in the blood of a Stygian ox, the Master drew a mystic character on the child's cheek, so he would be capable of bellowing great distances. Finally the Master tickled the boy's left foot and twisted the baby's right ear, so the child might move listeners to tears and laughter.

"May your son bless the Guild as we have blessed him today," the Guildmaster told the new parents.

Johan shook his superior's hand. His pale face flushed with unavoidable pride. Rose, his wife, was bent over the street pump in front of the house, washing chicken blood from her hands. The child had leached some of her meager beauty, but her blonde hair still shone with the luster of pregnancy.

"The entrails of the chicken were most propitious," she told the two men. "Ann of the Shadows said they were some of the most gaseous she had ever seen at a Guild birth-blessing."

"May the gods be generous to your son and to our Guild," Simon said.

"Amennn," the parents answered together.

After hours of festivity, the last pitchers of harvest beer flowed down the practiced throats of the Guild members and the celebration tables were cleared of food. It had been a joyous day and, given the modest means of Johan and Rose, a robust celebration.

Finally the whole Guild of Seers, Speakers, Dreamers, Storytellers, and Non-Fanatical Prophets and their families left the narrow, thatched house and ambled to their more substantial residences. As was the custom, Simon the Guildmaster brought up the rear. When he turned from Sparrow Alley to the Boulevard of the Muses, he heard the strident, powerful cries of the baby. Simon took it as good omen and smiled.

Remus, as the child was named, rapidly outstripped his father's abilities. Johan was a second-level singer; the Guild used him for Informal Gatherings, Name Day

Celebrations, Duck Pin Tournaments and the like. Though his enthusiasm exceeded his skill, the Guild made good use of Johan with serfs and artisans. Suffice it to say that Johan was not accredited for Large Public Gatherings or Castle Entertainment.

Already, in the Guild pre-school, Remus displayed remarkable voice and, despite his youth, was an admirable bearer of tales. His robust frame and black spiky burr of hair were in marked contrast to the frailty of his blonde parents. The malicious whispered about the barbarian mercenary levy that had taken place in Smunsk some months before Remus's birth, when Johan left his young wife to go on a tour of yak drivers' stations in the provinces. But most shared the attitude of Simon the Guildmaster, who saw the first wisps of shadow-making skills in the boy and knew the deep love Johan and Rose had for the child, whatever his earthly (or as some whispered) daemonic origins. And Simon also saw in the child the possibilities of fame for the Guild and his own reputation as a teacher. In the puffed ambitions of the good Guildmaster, we now recognize the power of dream-planting that Remus could work at even this young age.

One summer evening, Johan and Remus sat on the stoop of the house telling stories to the urchins of Sparrow Alley. Tongue work, Johan called it and knew it good practice for his teen-aged son. Caught up in the potent focus of their unlined faces, the grey-haired little man sketched fairy tales and mild hauntings for the generous currency of their attention. At last Johan blew the candle out, ceased his finger pictures of ogres, birds, and rabbits, picked up the candle holder, and went inside.

"Might I stay out and practice on the children?" Remus asked his father.

"Practice WITH the children," Johan corrected, secretly pleased at his son's request. Johan understood the boy's desire to work without his father present.

"As you wish, Remus. But I'll call you in soon. Don't start an epic."

Remus and his audience sat and listened as Johan went upstairs. Some nights the old man feigned his departure and listened to his son from the hallway. Those nights Remus had to watch what stories he told, staying with the stale, moralizing fables that the Guild ordained as proper for young audiences.

But tonight Remus was free to experiment.

"He's gone," Remus said, "now I'll tell REAL stories. Pay."

The children on the stoop began emptying their pockets: coins, small bits of jewelry from the back drawer of a mother's dowry trove, silver forks, even a tiny cured ham. Remus looked over the gifts, put them smoothly into his leather study sack, eyed the uneasy children.

"Some of these are cheap offerings..."

The children shivered.

" . . . but I'm feeling kind."

They let their breath out in relief.

"If you want to hear more, next time I expect greater reward," Remus told them, shaking the sack for emphasis. "Do we understand each other?" A mewing sibilance of agreement from the children. "We'd best start; the old fool will call me in a minute. So listen to me now."

The children, who had been fidgeting in anticipation, froze. Indeed they had no choice. The nights Remus spent on the stoop with them had gradually revealed some of his powers to himself. Remus slipped into each mind with tendrils of command as soft and binding as root filaments. He found the stagnant pools, the cellars, keeps, and closets within each child, and he let some of their denizens loose. Just enough to make each listener vulnerable. Remus judged his control now by the drawn bows of parted lips.

Remus smiled in faint scorn and began: "Once there was a frog who hoped to be a prince and there was also a cruel princess who had heard of the frog's dream . . . ''

Remus drew an emerald tree frog from his jerkin pocket, pulled a long steel needle from his belt. He held the supple frog by its feet; the frog jerked in futile parody of jumping. Though he never needed them, Remus had a fondness for props.

When Johan finally called Remus to bed, the children stumbled home, their faces drained and flat. The images faded from their memories; the fears that Remus had released drew slowly back. Though they stayed out beyond bedtime when Remus told them stories, their parents never complained: the children slept like the dead. Upon waking, all spoke of the beauty of Remus's stories, though none could quite remember them. And other than this just appreciation, there were no effects that any noticed. Just the waxing vague hunger that in the evenings drew more and more of the children of Smunsk to Sparrow Alley to hear the stories that Remus told on the stone steps of his father's house.

At sixteen Remus was a rangy, handsome youth with a studied sullenness. In the Guild Hall, Master Simon had taken over his exclusive instruction. Remus had sped through the minor orders of memory, gesture, improvisation, and flattery and now stood just two ranks below his father, an unprecedented achievement that gave the older man only pride.

Simon sat at the stained carved lectern that loomed over the Guild Hall like the figurehead of a spectral ship. From this eminence, he oversaw the day-long classes that filled the immense room, bellowing out corrections through the din and gabble of voices. Classes were taught simultaneously, the Guild instructors agreeing that any speaker must be capable of conquering the noisy distraction of other raised voices. Now at twilight, the final class of the day, the politicians, strove to hone their slippery craft. These students were, for the most part, talentless adolescents from wealthy families, whose instruction produced an embarrassingly large portion of the Guild's income.

As a class-ending drill, Tipple, the Master, was putting his charges through the daily Broad Gesture exercises.

"Watch me," he commanded, "it's a wide sweep, not a mincing hack."

Tipple swung one meaty, beringed hand and accidentally hit a student bent over in ursine Erstwhile Listening. The rest of the class guffawed and choked on their cigars.

Simon shook his head and walked out into the evening.

The pathetic nature of the class accentuated the gifts of Remus, Johan's son.

And what would the boy become, Simon mused. His skills were so prodigious that the future shot out in countless arcs. Remus's natural artistry made him shun politics. But Simon had also seen the hunger that Remus had for an audience, a hunger that completely counterfeited what all true storytellers possessed: the urge to speak and share; to fuse tale, teller, time, and listeners in one ephemeral union.

Sometimes Simon himself was disconcerted by Remus, the youth seeming to mock him without actually doing so. Perhaps Remus's glib, arch manner came from never being extended or challenged. But Simon sensed in an inchoate, disquieting way that there was a coldness in the marrow of this almost too talented stripling. Too often, Simon had heard Remus shift the focus of the listeners from the story to himself, watched as in barely perceptible ways the boy eased communication to control. The Master had tried to inculcate Remus with the classic lessons of the seduction of power, of the gifted and the fame-graced brought low, robbed by indolence and adulation of the very talent that had raised them. But Remus parroted back the morals of these illustrative fables with an oily comprehension that bespoke only understanding.

Simon wandered through the marketplace, where the farmers packing their unsold produce back into the ox carts grinned as they saw the old man gesturing into the darkening sky. The artist snared by a story. And indeed he was, though the story in Simon's heart grew more and more disturbing: Remus a Leader, a Major Entertainer, or even a Mesmerist.

Fortunately, Mesmerists only appeared once or twice a century. The last had led the youth of the whole Six Kingdoms in a weaponless crusade against the Insatiable Trolls of the Icy Moors.

Simon's immediate concern was the boy's forthcoming public examination by audience. To be admitted as a full member of the Guild of Seers, Speakers, Dreamers, Storytellers, and Non-Fanatical Prophets of Smunsk, a candidate must entertain an audience drawn by public crier and move them to applause. Never had a candidate so young been offered to the fickle reception of the crowd.

And the story itself that the candidate told was the deeper part of the test. For each candidate must go out into the wide world and find a new story or a shining variation of an old one. Thus the Guild itself was enriched and the trove of its spoken knowledge increased by each successful applicant. Though Guild members learned hundreds of stories throughout their careers, it was this quest story that truly defined each artist, that each became known for. It was Guild Law that name credit be given whenever a quest story was told by another.

Listeners were always hungry for unheard adventures, fairy tales, and fantastical diversions. Some few times, a quest story became the immediate fortune of its discoverer. Word of the story's beauty, power, or vision would spread in a fever throughout the Six Kingdoms, and only the tale told with the integrity of its master's voice would satisfy the munificent curiosity of even rulers and their courts.

In its own way, the search for a new story was as arduous or dangerous as the trial by audience. Some candidates vanished for years before returning with stale limericks; some gave up and took their revenge on listeners by becoming salesmen. Though the times were relatively tranquil, some died in the course of their travels from hunger, ill-health, or banditti.

Often, the quest itself became fabled and was told with the quest tale or even supplanted it. So it was that the delicate myth of the elves and how they came to forge the snowflakes was incomplete without the preface of how Zubon had heard the story through the gossamer walls of a Lutner bawdy house. All that was remembered of Glagno's story was the search itself: the oar-bondage for twelve years in the benches of the Choline Pirate flagship, the mermaid's love for him, and how the waterspout drew the two of them up to reign in the Mistral until the final drying of the seas.

With like tales, aphorisms, and nuggets of sleep-inducing advice, Johan prepared his son that rain-soaked, mist-bedraggled morning when Remus set out in search of the story that was to be his fortune. Remus lolled with undisguised boredom as his father gave him the last words of paternal advice:

"And never begrudge listening to the poorest, most unlikely speaker. Some of the finest stories in the Guild's history have come from toothless mouths and vacant faces. My own story I found by listening . . . "

" . . . to a leech-gatherer who mumbled it to you from the mud of a bog in a thunderstorm," Remus concluded, having heard the story of his father's story innumerable times.

"I know you've heard it all before, Remus," said his father, "and that's the lot and bane of all sons."

He clapped him sharply on the shoulder. "Be gone,

boy, be gone and be well. Write to your mother, if you get a chance. And remember to display the seeker's Medallion on your chest. It'll guard you from harm and draw those who would speak to you.''

Remus tapped the Medallion on his son's cloak with reverent nostalgia. A tongue of fire embroidered with gold threads, Rose had spent hours making this emblem of her son's quest. The medallion was mark of protection; anyone in the Six Kingdoms harming the tale-seeker would be killed with leisurely, agonizing torture by the local Guild. Many miscreants committed suicide rather than enduring the torment of listening to a Guild member chant the genealogy of famous pig breeds or the coronation speeches of their monarchs. But while the badge shielded one from physical danger, it also drew drudges and bores to the Guild candidate, those who were full of private wisdom, family japes, and bathhouse-wall canards.

''Good-bye, father,'' Remus said with transparent eagerness. ''I'll return with a story that will bathe me in jewels.''

They exchanged the secret handclasp of the Guild and Remus leaped down from the steps and walked through the stale shadows and dripping eaves of Sparrow Alley. He swung onto the Boulevard of the Muses and headed swiftly for the city gates, for the wide world beyond the walls of Smunsk.

Without looking, Remus sensed Simon the Guildmaster quietly gazing from a rain-streaked window of the Guild Hall. Simon had awakened hours before class to watch his prize student depart. Remus reached the strong gaze of his mind-sight into the old man's soul, laughed to himself at the ambition and affection for him that fused in the old man's heart, and sent a prickly, hobbling gasp of arthritis through the Guildmaster. With a jaunty lope, Remus passed through the city gates, nodded graciously as the guards saluted the Guild Medallion glowing on his cloak. He walked off into the distance, the muddy road sucking at his boots.

Though he was but sixteen, Remus was broad-shouldered, strong, and confident, wise beyond his years with the pilfered wisdom of the many whose memories he had slipped into without their knowledge. The power of his thought-thievery had grown mightily in the last months. Only his parents and a few others had thwarted his inner prying. There was a kindness to Rose and Johan that was repellent. Some fewer were opaque with the sheer force of their thoughts. Already he could read the eyes of women, and he sought behind the eyes with the mind-vision he exercised with such power. And contrary to Guild custom of poverty for story searchers, Remus carried a weighty store of coins frightened from the hordes of children who had begged his stories each night in Sparrow Alley.

Remus pulled the Guild Medallion off his cloak. With his powers he didn't need it. He'd sift through those he met until he found a story dazzling in its invention and take it as his own without its possessor's knowledge. A week or two to gain the tale, a month or two of pleasure in the towns and then he'd have some wench sew the Medallion back on his cloak and he'd return to his Guild fortune. Remus walked on, oblivious of the rain, spending the wealth of his fabulous future, warmed by the certainty of his triumph.

After a month of drunken dalliance, of utter confidence in his thought-thievery, Remus realized that he had found nothing worth repeating. He was cautious of openly cheating those he met, of mentally forcing them to give him money. His fortune of childbooty melted away. He began to search in earnest.

While he was by no means humbled, Remus had been brought to a grudging admission. The Guild quest was a greater challenge than he had ever imagined. His mind-reading had almost worked against him; it had brought an almost immediate recognition of how rare a truly original story was. Every story that he sapped and fleeced from an unsuspecting mind was a variation of ones he had heard spoken in the Guild many times, had learned in the simplest classes.

With deepening worry, Remus realized that all the stories might have been found, that he might be living in a barren, lightless age in which conventional wisdom had driven out the capacity for wonder that made stories possible. That there were no new stories left. There were many tale bearers, but no tale crafters. And Remus did not desire a mere minor myth, some tiny cameo of elvish magics; he desperately sought something beyond mere uniqueness: a work of such chilling originality that it would be a miracle that it not be known.

He finally moved out of the cities, the villages, and hamlets, where true story-speaking had slipped to gossip and listening was unheard of. If there were any tales left, Remus knew he must find them in the countryside, in superstition-tainted hollows, around the fires of wanderers and nomads, for whom the sun still had a name and the wind a voice. With these people, he could prompt a rude bed and a simple meal as he mined their pagan thoughts for that rarest jewel, a story of magnitude and undiscovered brilliance.

It was a bitter day at the end of the third month of Remus's quest. The ground was hard with frost. It had been five days since he left the piled turf lodges of the wolf-hunters, two days since he had exhausted the store of jerky and flat bread they had given him. He was numb from the impassive roof of grey winter clouds, the ceaseless, leaching wind, from probing the minds of the hunters. The hunters had had no myths or stories, barely thoughts, only a savage and precise series of sexual fantasies, some of which involved women. The unrelenting weather had an elemental purity that he found almost preferable to the hunters' dreams.

Remus saw smoke rise from deep within the winter-barren forest and be torn to nothingness by the wind. He stumbled into the nameless woods and dreamed vaguely of thawing himself and mind-tinkering a meal from whomever he met. He found a faint trail that seemed to bend toward the smoke. He hoped it led to whatever tended the fire and the warmth it promised. Be it troll, brigand, or simple woodcutter, Remus was beyond caring.

Hunger stitched pain in his belly. Jackdaws and ravens flapped away as he followed the suggestion of the path, were snatched away by the gusts like leaves of a black autumn. The trees stood closer together and the stony halflight of the day darkened. Remus stumbled on, wished blankly that he reach the fire and whatever fate awaited before night left him blind and alone for the prowling beasts of the forest. Remus's ambitions had simplified to a steaming bowl and the mindless company of dancing flames.

Remus was about to throw himself on the ground and become one more lost story when he cleared a rise and, with night seeming to pause for a moment on the spikes of the bare treetops, looked down into a tiny clearing and saw a hearth fire winking through the walls of a glass house.

"Welcome, storyteller," a caressing, cinnamon voice said barely above the wind. "It is time that we finally meet."

A small, humped figure stepped out of the twilight. It was a hunchbacked crone, the hollow socket of her left eye sewn shut with golden thread, thread like that of Remus's mother-sewn Medallion. She reached out a withered hand, took his arm and led him into the shining rooms of the glass house.

Remus awoke in the middle of the night. The bowl of venison stew and the warmth of the fire had melted him to weariness, and the crone had led him to a small room where he had fallen asleep on a simple, sumptuous pile of furs. Now he lay awake and watched the stars winking through the clarity of the glass roof. Remus rolled over and saw the fire in the hearth fallen to a red honeycomb. A soft, strong light rippled from a corner of the living room beyond the fireplace. Remus stared and in the cold radiance recognized the old woman's face, saw how light issued from her open mouth as she slept, broke like silent water over her knees, and gradually faded across the floor.

Remus realized that he slept in the house of a witch, a storyteller whose very breath was luminous with soul-shivering power. Such were the legends that he had laughed at in the Guild School. Only exhaustion let him regain sleep. At that moment Remus knew he had found his story and his fortune.

Rain bathed the glass house the next morning, gave way to broken clouds and finally an austerity of winter sun. The crone quietly went about her household tasks, as she watched him devour the elegant meals that she materialized with slashes of her crabbed hands. Remus smiled back winsomely and tried to pry inside her mind. The first feathery attempt to slip into her thoughts drove a spike of pain through his forehead. He recoiled and knew that he must wait.

The shadows of the bare trees crept in long fingers through the transparent walls before she finally spoke. Once more Remus was startled by the contrast between the limpid, effortless beauty of her voice and the ruin of her body. She sat down on the opposite side of the crystal table, glanced at him with the disconcerting nakedness of her one maelstrom eye.

"Enough hesitation and sparring, my dear," she said soothingly. "My name is Mali, Mali of the Moonfire Tongue. I know of your quest and your vaunting ambitions. I too have needs and desires. Rarely have I met one so young with such mind force. So young and so handsome."

"Thank you," Remus said politely, "I wait on your

words, oh paragon of beauty and kindness."

Her dry lips twitched in an unfortunate display of her gums. "I am happy that fate conspired to unite the two of us. You see, I am dying."

"I'm sorry," Remus volunteered with admirable sympathy.

"And before I die, I would pass some of my craft to one worthy of receiving it."

Remus tensed involuntarily as a foxfire of eagerness played over him.

"Or more honestly," the crone continued, in the honeyed youth of her voice, "I would trade with you. I offer you a story, a story that is my heart's essence. A never-heard story that would be the making of your glory. I know you saw the light well from my mouth last night. You sense the core of my being. And in your marrow, you know I speak the truth."

Remus quickly bobbed his head, leaned forward on his elbows. "It is no belief I have in you, it is certitude," he said. Then he pulled out his dirk, pinked his little finger. "Make what trade you will. I offer my blood."

The two watched the blood pool on the icy table. Then the hag laughed. "Dying, I desire not your death, manling. I want less than your blood. Less and more." She touched his finger and healed it.

The anticipation of his future dragged Remus headlong to words. "I agree to your terms, oh fey and generous lady."

"I am glad that we avoid unseemly haggling," she said softly. "There are but two sticking points. The first is that you must whisper thanks to me three times before each telling you make of the story. These small thanks will sustain my soul in its lonely wanderings after death.''

"Most readily, willingly agreed," Remus hastened.

"The last condition is simply this: you must sleep with me this night and love me to my satisfaction. If my tongue is quickened to joy, I will give you my story at night's end.''

The crone finally broke the lingering silence.

"Brave words you spoke before you heard my price," her shining voice quavered. "I do not hold you to your too-eager promise.''

Remus suppressed a shudder before his hand stroked her dank hair. He bent across the table, pulled her face to his and felt her tongue slide between his lips.

The moon rose and fell, the stars spun in their courses, and Remus watched them slowly toll the night away through the crystal thatch of the glass house. His senses blurred to nightmare. Remus slid down the glistening cries of her voice and finally ceased to wonder at the voracious fecundity of her desire.

Somehow through the wall he heard the bird cries that presage dawn. He found himself on the floor, awakening at Mali's feet. Every joint ached and his mouth tasted of compost. The old woman rocked gently in her rocking chair, humming to herself, beams of light breaking through her gape-tooth smile like stalks of golden wheat.

"Well and most prodigally done, my final love," the beautiful voice purred. "Bargain made, price paid. Rest your head on my grateful thighs, and I will give you the story that is my life.''

And she rocked and stroked Remus's head as it rose and fell on the withered sea of her thighs. And the voice, which held all the beauty that the woman's body lacked, lulled him and loved him again. Light fell from her mouth like a dazzling rope, like the cord between mother and newborn. The light fell from her mouth and flowed between the narrow parting of his lips and filled Remus with the heady distillation of dreams. And this is the story she told him: the Tale of the Dragon.

IN THOSE AUGUST YEARS, WHEN the air itself was more substantial and supported them more easily and the stronger darkness gave richer contrast to their flames, a dragon of promising wing span, potent breath, and teeth of admirable sharpness was born in the high peaks of the Dolorous Mountains.

Her parents watched the pearly egg crack, saw the ruby eggtooth pierce the opalescent shell. Balog, the male, breathed spurts of smoke as Falla, his mate, crouched over the emerging dragonette. Falla's neck snaked back and forth as she cocked her python head. Her crystalline eyes throbbed jade to ruby, fear to love. It was their first hatch.

Two hundred yards below the eyrie, wedged into a narrow fissure of the adamantine cliffs, Kazan the thief heard the signals of breath, spied the gouts of fire and steam that broke across the upper ledges. He realized that his agonies of preparation would soon bring him wealth or death. No man of the Shattered Coasts had ever stolen a dragon chick.

Her scaly udders distended with mother's magma, Falla dragged herself to the nest of gold coins, jewels, and men's bones that she and Balog had fashioned from the heaped store of their cave. As she fell to her side, Falla drew the wobbly newborn to her teats with a gentle wing. Balog licked the tender scales of his mate's neck, and Falla lifted her wing to show the fierce nursing.

Balog growled with satisfaction and turned to the mouth of the cave, his claws striking sparks on the stone floor. Twelve leagues distant, there was a village of Amazons that Balog had spared for this event. Tonight he would return with some of the tender warriors in his craw for Falla. Balog flapped open the leather of his wings, blew one spurting triumph of conflagration, and sprang from the cliff into flight.

The vast cold shadow passed over Kazan as he crouched against the cliff, his face and hair darkened with ashes to the complexion of the rock. He watched the male fly with baleful swiftness away, away. After five still minutes, Kazan gently opened his pack and readied himself.

In the cavern above, the dragon nestled against her mother's breasts, her small snake head shiny-scaled. Faint rings of smoke broke over the perfect daggers of her teeth. When her daughter fell asleep satiated, Falla drifted to shallow, grateful rest.

At the top of the rock chimney, Kazan pressed his feet against the far wall and wedged himself cautiously. He flexed his bruised hands over and over until they felt supple again, drew five deep, silent breaths, and flung himself up.

As he cast himself over the rim of the cliff, the smouldering half-closed eyes of the mother beast flared open, the cleft wet whip of her tongue flickered out, and she bellowed to her feet. Kazan yanked the horn bow from his shoulder, notched the silver-headed arrow, in a heartbeat drew it back and shot the cured thornwood shaft through the fiery left eye and into the abomination's brain.

Falla blasted one wail of fire over the small figure, but Kazan had turned his back and the wizard-blessed leather singed, cracked, and held. Falla's stubby feet scrabbled at the rock, and she died before her head thudded at Kazan's feet. Her tail slashed three times, flung treasure and bones against the walls of the cave. Kazan turned slowly as the dust of the lair settled on him. There were only two sounds: his breathing and the puling, urgent cries of the baby dragon.

Kazan unwrapped the drugged goat's heart and forced it between the jaws of the monstrous infant. She swallowed it in one frightful bite. Kazan watched the lump slide down the amber throat. The baby's eyes glowed at him with predatory affection. As Kazan returned to his pack at the edge of the cliff, the dragonette waddled after him, nuzzling his legs and hissing for affection. By the time Kazan had uncoiled the vine rope, the tiny beast had curled in leaden sleep, her head pointed toward her new parent. Kazan stared fitfully into the sky. He needed another hour. Tying one end around the dead beast's neck, Kazan played the thin, steely rope down the long rock face until he felt it slacken.

Using catgut thongs, Kazan bound together the legs of his prize. With the tenderness of all thieves for priceless goods, he slid the sleeve of dragon skin over the sleeping chick, drew his steal-sack barely shut to admit air. Kazan forced the bag into his pack, squatted to pull the straps over his shoulders, wobbled to his feet. The months of exercise had strengthened him; though the dragonette was almost his weight, Kazan could carry her.

The rope cinched around him; Kazan stared for the last time at the dragon's lair, at the mounds of jewels and coin, at the skulls studding the floor. The great scales of the mother dragon were already beginning to darken and fade. He thought of her mate, shivered, and began to rappel down the grim precipice. By the time he reached the base of the cliff, his hands were bloody from the speed of his descent. Kazan ignored the pain. The sure knowledge of his fate if he were caught spilled through his thoughts. He tightened the straps of the pack and set off at a desperate trot for the tiny mouth of the Endless Caverns. It was a league and a half away.

Even before the proof of sight, Balog felt there was something horribly, inexplicably wrong. The sky itself stank with the treachery of humankind, and when he saw the awkward cast of Falla's body at the mouth of their cavern, he knew the tragedy as he skidded across the floor of their nesting place. He swallowed the now-bitter bits and blood of the Amazons that he would have coughed down his nursing wife's throat, saw the serpentine glory of her body stiffened, their firstborn gone, stolen, seized; the hateful shaft in his mate's once-burning eye and, most sacrilegious, the mother used as anchor for the violator's rope. Later he would eat her body, as blood and love demanded, but now Balog was lover and father-avenger. The flame of his hatred blackened the cave, and he turned in cold, fiery wrath to the rescue of their firstborn. Balog hung steel-taloned on the brow of the cliff, and his keen nostrils defined the smell of the thief. He glided swiftly to the base of the mountain, caught the scent again, rose relentless and inexorable to skim the rock barrens, massive and deathgrim, to rescue his child, to rend the murderer and thief of his happiness.

Moments away, he found them: the wretched little figure bent beneath a burden that must be his daughter. The creature turned a frightened, white face as Balog swept down with spread claws. And then it vanished into a tiny hole in the rocks. Balog's talons scored the opening, and he crashed and scrambled to the hole, thrust his snapping jaws in as far as his neck could reach, heard the thief scuttling deep away, the baby's scales too soft for him to use flames.

His claws were blunted; blood from his foot pads seared the cave mouth. It was a day and a night before Balog admitted her loss. His heart was as bitter and black as the taunting darkness of this thief's entrance. Balog spread his wings and flew to wreak his woeful vengeance on men and all their works.

Blind hours of stumbled tunnels, of the way anxiously divined in the flicker of a sputtering torch, Kazan's attention fixed on the smears of glow-worm paste that marked the single proper path in the labyrinthine confusion of the galleries and tunnels of the Endless Caverns. A misstep, a false turn, and Kazan and his prize would be forever lost in the lightless gullet of the indifferent rocks.

But as his legs trembled with exhaustion, the pack squirming on his shoulders, Kazan recognized the quartz knob at the entrance to his refuge and stumbled into the perpetual light of the vast gallery. Slipping off the pack, he gently drew the mewing dragon from its sheath, clamped the twice-forged manacle about her neck, and, shielding his face from the sear of heat, led her to the great chain anchored in the living rock. He fastened her manacle to it with a troll-proof padlock whose key hung from a leather strap around his neck. The chain was long enough to reach to the cleft deep within which throbbed the magma that gave the huge gallery its constant illumination. Here the dragon could feed on the fire-milk that would nourish it in the weeks of solitary training that lay ahead. The beast rasped Kazan's face once with her tongue, then ambled off to feed at the end of her chain.

Spent, Kazan stumbled to the far side of the chamber, unfolded the dragon-skin suit that he must forever wear to mask his man-scent from the dragon's natural appetite for humankind, slid into its stiff folds, pulled a goat bladder of Scythean honey wine from his pile of stores, and drank a self-satisfied toast to his audacity and glittering future. He fell into the first untroubled sleep he had had in months.

Kazan named her Almara. As goslings will bind themselves to a dog or a man in the absence of true parents, so Almara clove to Kazan. In the three months in the cave, the she-dragon grew rapidly. Kazan raised her with calculating kindness, preening the strengthening wings, polishing her scales with fleece, and trimming her nails with great armor files. Occasionally he fed her bits of the dried corpses of the three beggars he had hired so stealthily to carry his provisions into the depths of the Endless Caverns. To keep his scheme secret, Kazan had killed them when they reached the gallery. Almara gnawed their hacked limbs with ravenous alacrity.

The dragon's love for him waxed and deepened as she grew. She never questioned their disparity. The last month in the cavern, Kazan could control her with his voice. She was flying now, swooping through the harsh, lava-lit heights of the gallery in the newly discovered pleasure of flight. They had taken to sleeping beside each other, Kazan awakening to find himself blanketed with the velvet stretch of her wing. He found that he enjoyed grooming her and was faintly puzzled at this slight softness in the splendor of his great and greedy scheme. Almara took well to saddle and bit; she seemed more eager to fly with him astride her neck than to fly alone. Kazan sighed in a surfeit of ambition as he stroked the warm muzzle, watched the steam of her breath break between the fingers of his blacksmith gloves. One week more of flame practice on the mannikins hung from the stalactites and they would be ready for the sun, for the kingdoms of men, for Kazan's ascension to wealth, more rightly, for the glint of sunlight on gold and a nest of bullion and jewels for Almara.

She followed him faithfully through the dark leagues of twisted caverns as Kazan obeyed the glowing trail marks he had left long months ago, the daubs of faint luminescence that led beneath the raw-edged snow-crested mountains that separated them from her long-forgotten parents' lair. Hopefully he was beyond her father's wrath. When at last the dragon and her master stood at the cavern mouth, each rejoiced at the sweep of the verdant fields and tiny order of the villages beneath them. Almara bent her head to Kazan's face, saw the avid hunger there and took it as her own. He scratched the tender scales above her eyes, tightened the saddle on her lowered neck, took the reins in his hands, and together they leaped into the waiting sky, the bountiful horizons of their future.

After five years of fighting dour battles, of crushing insurrections, scattering invaders, or simply leveling recalcitrant villages and obdurate castles, Kazan was rich. His coffers were full, his tables groaned, his lands produced plentifully. He had a grim castle, his own wizard. Kazan was bored.

Kazan the King-Maker, Worm-Lord, and Fire-Wielder listened with faint interest to the proposition of the emissary of Udo the Malignant. The round, sweaty man spoke with a sincerity that testified that his life was forfeit if he could not enlist the infallible assistance of the Dragon Master:

"And in his further generosity, Lord Udo offers the hand of his only daughter to the wondrous Kazan, most glorious wreaker of havoc, army destroyer . . ."

"Cease," Kazan ordered from his winged throne. "Grolsch, what is the measure of this Udo?"

The desiccated wizard stepped from behind the throne and spoke in a bored voice, "A poisoning, cutpurse, whoreson greedy rogue who usurped his father's throne and mounted his mother to have this daughter.''

"Not another," Kazan sighed in disgust. "Away, serf.''

"And Lord Udo begged that you peruse this limning of Princess Fiona," the little man wheedled as he drew an icon from his diplomatic pouch.

The small picture glowed less from its artistry than its subject. Perhaps it was the golden sheen of the hair, but Kazan leaned forward with a certain hunger. The messenger stammered up the steps, handed the picture to Kazan with abject hope.

"Is this a true likeness?" Kazan asked the wizard, passing him the image.

Grolsch twisted the picture in his taloned hands, held the painting close to his hard eyes, seemed to peer down the maiden's bosom.

"Strangely enough, yes," he said. "There is a certain timid magic to the colors, but this truly is the girl."

He handed it back to Kazan, who studied the miniature a long moment.

"She's a virgin," the messenger added redundantly.

Grolsch snorted. Kazan glared at the little man, then turned the picture face down in his lap.

"We'll subdue Lord Udo's populace," Kazan said abruptly. "Fifty per cent down, fifty per cent upon completion, the Princess on my arrival. Grolsch will draw up the usual contract with you.''

A bellow of scorching longing surged from the courtyard, shook the tapestries along the high walls, thrummed through the stones of the castle.

"Gentlemen, you must excuse me. My mistress calls." Kazan gave them both an ironic bow, strode through the great hall, his dragon livery creaking.

As she always did when Kazan walked into the courtyard, Almara squealed joyously and blew flame into the evening air. In the intervals between battles, they flew daily together at dawn and dusk.

Almara was fully grown now, the length of twenty tall men from black snout to lashing tip of her arrowhead tail. Her scales were darkly iridescent, her wings had the sheen of a dark lake, testimony to her health and the delicate, exclusive care that Kazan gave her. The Dragon Master himself still groomed, polished, stroked, and preened her.

And Kazan still wore the dragon-skin suit. He was weary of its stiff embrace. He even slept in it. But Grolsch had confirmed for him its absolute necessity. Kazan himself had eye-proof of Almara's appetites as he watched her take her bloating fill of the race of man after each conflict. Fortunately, she was fastidious, and as was her gentle wont, licked him only after cleaning herself of the scraps of her meals.

Almara lowered her great head to have him scratch behind her ears. Her lambent eyes glittered; she allowed no one else near her. The months of training in the cavern had made her Kazan's. Kazan sensed more and more in those first turbulent years, as she protected her frail rider from arrows and lances, that Almara regarded him as hers and fought with even deeper fury the few times he had been wounded. Even the treachery, machinations, and intrigues of the jealous were forestalled by the knowledge of the dragon's wrathful affection.

Now as they mounted the evening sky, Kazan saw the first stars glinting to light and thought of Fiona, and dreamt, as even rich thieves do, of marrying a princess. A cold wind buffeted the dragon and Kazan slid a little in the saddle. Almara looked back quickly, saw his hand wave assurance. Satisfied, she blew one long gust of fire into the rising darkness.

Singed, smoke-soiled and sweaty, Kazan slid from the dragon's back and strode wearily across the jousting field in front of Udo's castle to the waiting awe-struck crowd and the cluster of ermine-clad nobility drawn apprehensively before them.

It had almost been too easy. The small village had withered beneath the torch of Almara's breath; the men had put up a desperate momentary resistance, and then Almara had eaten, barely staunching her hunger. Apparently the villagers had refused to pay Udo's last usurious tax. The collection of Udo's levies would be much smoother now, Kazan thought.

The band struck up a disjointed march, the ranks of ragged soldiers snapped to attention, and Udo the Malignant waddled out to meet Kazan. A small, veiled maiden followed in his wake. Grolsch walked solemnly behind the pair.

"Well done. Oh, most completely, horribly successful," the greasy little man gushed, adjusting his coronet. "My deepest, most heartfelt thanks, oh mighty Lord Kazan. Even now the other villages hurry their late taxes to our humble gates."

"Grolsch," Kazan asked, "has our fee been paid?"

"Loaded into your coaches and sped to Castle Kazan," bowed the wizard.

"Even so," said Udo, his eyes shiny with porcine hospitality, leading the girl forward. At Udo's nudge, she dropped her veil. A blush suffused her flawless face as Kazan stared in disbelief at the palpable innocence of her.

"We have prepared a modest feast in your honor and that of your bride," Udo said, with a bow "and have laid out the wedding chamber."

The child blushed even deeper, seemed on the edge of tears.

Kazan looked at the wizard in mild confusion.

"The fat wretch wishes to be able to say that you are his son-in-law," Grolsch explained. "We can take her now without further delay."

The beautiful child began to cry.

"It is as your wizard says," Udo agreed. "My daughter is yours to do with as you please. I merely suggested the marriage vows to make her more compliant to your wishes."

Castle Kazan was not a particularly festive place. Perhaps it was best to have their first night here, Kazan thought. He shrugged. "If it will put the girl at ease, we will have a marriage ceremony."

Without speaking, the Princess Fiona reached out and took Kazan's smoky hand in both of hers.

Across the field, the dragon Almara suddenly bellowed and tore the earth as the girl touched Kazan. Udo, Fiona, and Grolsch stepped away from the Dragon Master.

"Ready the marriage feast, Lord Udo," ordered Kazan. "I will settle the dragon for the night and then return to minister to my betrothed."

All hastened into the castle. Kazan hurried to the restive dragon, stroked her hot muzzle, took the saddle from her neck, led her into the depths of the granary under the castle walls, chained her to the thick millstones. Almara threw herself on the cobbled floor with a clatter of scales and watched Kazan with a fitful flickering in her jeweled eyes.

"Still hungry, sweet friend?" Kazan asked.

He scratched behind her tiny, tufted ears. The dragon growled faintly.

"It's away tomorrow, you and I, back to our castle. I weary of these pitiful escapades. We must get out of politics and back to honest thievery."

The dragon gave him a brief nuzzle, rolled away. Kazan stroked her neck.

"Good night, faithful beast," he said as he walked out. He remembered the face of the princess and lengthened his stride.

Despite the slight smell of decay in the chapel of the local deity, the wedding had been moving. After they had exchanged vows, Princess Fiona, now wife to Kazan Dragon Lord, slipped the bridal veil from her face and let it drift to the floor. With fervent simplicity, she turned to her new master and embraced him. They were strangely matched: the child-bride in her white, intricate lace and the battle-lean thief in his hacked and worn dragon skin. The company cheered as the two walked out of the chapel to host the wedding feast, the bride's hair like beaten gold in the light of the ceremonial torches, the dry lisp of the groom's steps as he walked in his scaled boots.

As they sat at the high table of the feast, to see and be seen, Fiona kissed her husband before the well-wishers. "Thus I begin my thanks for saving me from that woesome beast," she told Kazan.

"The dragon is total servant to my wishes," Kazan assured her.

"Not the flying worm, dear husband. My father." She squeezed his hand with small, sharp-nailed fingers.

Fiona steadied her husband as they followed the wavering torches up the twisting staircase to the bridal chamber. Kazan had been obliged to drink numerous toasts. But he drew himself up when the castle steward opened the burnished door with its intricate castings of intertwined couples. The steward bowed to the bride and groom, handed Kazan the key to the door, and took himself away with discreet dispatch.

Kazan bent down in smirking bravado, caught the beauteous Fiona in his arms, and carried her across the threshold into the perfumed chamber. As her arms slowly tightened around his neck and he felt the petals of her breath, he glanced about the circular room. With its confection of white sheets and heaped pillows, the massive four-poster bed glowed in the swaying light of priapic candles set on high sticks of ebony. A ceiling-to-floor mirror doubled the bed and candles in its silvered depths. And beyond the bed stood a black cast-iron tub with four clawed feet and steam rising above its dark rim.

Plush towels and fragrant soaps rested on a small table beside it. Kazan stopped his kiss, stared momentarily. His bride caught the direction of his eyes, turned in his arms, and looked over to the tub.

"I ordered the servants to prepare these ablutions, my sweet lord," Fiona explained softly. "Before we attend to our mutual pleasure, I want to bathe your winsome body and myself wash the battle sweat from you. Would you love me like a lizard all in your scaly skin?" She laughed and began to undo the dull ivory dragon-tooth buttons that bound the suit to Kazan.

Kazan had taken his sporadic dalliance in brief interludes away from the dragon. His reservations died when Fiona put her mouth to the blanched skin of his chest as she slowly peeled the dragon garb from him.

"My lord tastes bitter," she said through puckered lips, "but I will sweeten him."

She drew the naked thief to the steaming tub, led his hands to the fastenings of her wedding gown and after the two stood bare as peeled sticks, they stepped together into the slow roiling of the scented waters. With wanton, blissful hands, Fiona washed five years of muck, dragon oils, and battle drear from Kazan's skin and made him smell like a man again.

The candles had guttered down to waxy fists when Kazan woke in those darkest moments before first light. Fiona, his wife, clung to him with tender possession as she slept, her hair snaking across the bed like rolling lava. During the night, his future had narrowed to the exquisite figure that lay beside him. His glance drifted over the mirror: the two languid bodies, the pillows tossed about the samite sheets like heaped clouds, the crimson swatches of his wife's virgin blood scattered across the milky, four-posted firmament.

His ear throbbed. Kazan reached up and felt the sticky warmth of his own blood on his fingers. It had passed without notice in the tumble of their love-making, but Kazan realized now that she had bitten through the lobe of his right ear.

Like the disquieting aftertaste of a troubled dream, Kazan sensed the dragon stirring, heard the low, demanding growl of his charge, lonely and hungry in the damp granary. He rose and silently pulled the dragon-skin suit onto himself again. After the bath and the gossamer pressure of Fiona's hands, his second skin had a chafing stiffness.

Heavy with wine and the fumes of love, Kazan stumbled down into the bowels of the castle, found the dragon crouched on her haunches, sheathing and unsheathing her claws. Almara flared her nostrils as he walked close, her eyes vortices of fire in the dark room.

"It is I, Kazan your Lord, oh worm of my heart, beast of my fortune," said the thief with a dull heartiness.

He picked her saddle off a pile of wheat sacks, threw it over her rigid neck, cinched it with practiced craft, tugged her reins lightly to lead her out. For the first time in Kazan's memory, the dragon resisted. He pulled harder, slipped, and almost fell in a puddle of her drool. Kazan lashed out with the reins and whipped her snout. Almara scuttled back, whimpered, and Kazan dropped the reins in embarrassment.

"Forgive my sharpness, dear Almara. My thoughts are elsewhere," Kazan apologized, stepping closer and scratching behind her ears.

After ten minutes of strokes and soft whispers, the simmering burble of Almara's breathing eased and Kazan led the reluctant dragon outside. Despite Almara's waking cries, Udo's castle remained silent. No doubt it was the earliness of the day and the effects of the wedding feast. Almara and Kazan stood in mute appreciation of the morning. The sun glowered at dawn's edge and the low sanguine beams pierced the ground fog in harmless mimicry of the dragon's battle wrath. Kazan swung into the worn comfort of the saddle, swayed in momentary giddiness. The dragon garb scraped against his flesh. The odor of the skin suit and the lucent soaps and rich oils of the nuptial bath mixed unpleasantly. The dragon glanced back at Kazan, wrinkled her nostrils, and turned away, a curious glimmer in the low embers of her eyes.

Kazan flicked the reins, and dragon and man mounted the air in swoops of her velveted wings. The castle of Udo the Malignant fell away, as in voiceless understanding they flew into the incarnadine simplicity of the rising light.

They soared for hours before returning so that the spirits of both man and dragon were once more in harmony as they wheeled above Udo's demesne. Suddenly the dragon drew its wings back and, stooping like a falcon, dove toward a milky flag flecked with a multitude of roseate butterflies, a flag that snapped above the castle's single tower, a tower that Kazan, clinging in numb confusion to the pommel of the dragon's saddle, realized held in its highest story the bridal chamber.

Almara tore a great swatch from the banner, worried it for a moment, swallowed the rag. Kazan pulled harshly at the bit, wondered anew at the antic behavior of his beast, and finally guided the dragon to a gentle landing at the far end of the jousting field. As Kazan sprang from the saddle in anger, Almara bowed her great head in contrition, a nervous slaver dribbling from her jaws. Kazan caught himself, eyed her with concern.

"Are you ill, my steed, my flying fortune," Kazan asked brusquely.

He touched her face, gave her ears a soft buffet. Almara licked his face, her black, cleft tongue rasping his skin.

Kazan stumbled back.

"Great clumsy beast," he cursed.

He touched the side of his head, stared at his bloody fingertips. The dragon had stripped the scab from the love bite Fiona had given his ear. Only the thud of the drawbridge falling across the moat drew his attention away and prevented him from berating his monstrous charge. The dragon herself crouched stolidly, the meek blaze of her eyes reflecting the image of Kazan.

Made familiar by Kazan's familiarity with his daughter, Count Udo walked with Grolsch and Fiona at the head of his festive court.

"A most sublime jest, Dragon Lord, a marvelous caprice," Udo told his son-in-law.

"You have my advantage," Kazan replied, with a flat courtesy engendered by Fiona's presence.

"Surely you were aware that the banner you directed your firedrake to rend was your wedding sheet, displayed by the bride's family as custom demands, fit testimony to her purity and your so-potent affection."

Kazan's silence was washed away in the jocund laughter of Udo's retainers. He glanced up to the torn sheet gaily flapping its speckled shreds from the flagstaff atop the wedding chamber, then looked with small embarrassment to his bride. Fiona wrinkled her nose, stepped to Kazan's side, and put her arm around his waist. "Let us leave swiftly, beloved liege and husband," she said.

Kazan noticed Fiona's attire for the first time. She wore a tight all-covering garment of sea-mist velvet, its surface lightly sketched with an intricacy of scales.

"My daughter heard of your dragon dress, Lord Kazan, and tormented me to have this likeness made for her once she knew her future was yours," Udo smiled indulgently. "We come out to bid you adieu and farewell. Your wizard says your services are bound already to another kingdom. And of course, farewell to a daughter, welcome to a new son," Udo bowed obsequiously to Kazan.

"Wholesale rates in the future," Grolsch said drily.

Kazan kissed Fiona over and again, held her at arm's length, admired the fit and sheen of her reptilian fashions. He led Fiona to the wizard, "Grolsch will speed you to the castle in his charmed carriage, my sweetest love."

Grolsch took her by the elbow as Kazan turned to the dragon.

The girl held her lover's steps with her voice, "May I not fly with you this once and only once?"

Kazan looked in bewilderment to the wizard, to the beseeching, heart-wrenching face of his bride, to the blue feather of a night heron plaited into her hair.

"The beast is tamed to your desires, my Lord," Grolsch volunteered. "Let the Lady Fiona ride only this one time. And besides," the wizard's face creased with an unexpected smile as he looked at the girl, "Love has its own wisdom."

Hand in hand, the Dragon Lord and his bride walked up

to the dragon. Kazan studied the creature's flat, expressionless face. Almara blinked at the tiny, golden-haired figure, then bent her great head for the girl to stroke. Kazan breathed again, sighed thanks.

"Oh dear and mighty Almara, you will carry my bride and me together to Castle Kazan. This is my wish and my command."

The dragon raised herself, enveloped them once in the dark shadow of her unfurled wings, and bowed her neck.

Kazan swung into the saddle, lifted his wife to sit before him, patted the glistening scales of his steed. Fiona waved a final time to the crowd and the dragon rose with awful majesty, left the groundlings in dusty turbulence.

When all could spy them again, the three were almost between clouds, a distant fabulous puppetry against the lighter sky. And then the tiny dragon shrugged and the lovers fell from their seat and a second, brighter sun novaed above Castle Udo. When the halos and furred light cleared from the vision of the momentarily blinded watchers, one smoking dragon-skin boot fell to earth, the blackened plume of a night heron drifted down in the warm drizzle of white ash.

Only a few had the presence of mind to follow Grolsch the wizard as he careened into the dank granary and burrowed deep into the mounds of unsavory grain. For Grolsch was the only one to realize that the fell dragon, grieving and heart-shattered, would return to feed.

Dawn's rosy fingers plucked at the cabin of glass. Mali's

voice rustled and cracked, narrowed to a trickle, "Some say it was the bridal bath that washed the dragon scent from Kazan and that when Almara tasted the blood of Kazan's love bite and smelled him for the first time as a man, the fate of the thief and the princess bride was sealed. Others feel it was the inevitable jealousy of the beast; that as long as Kazan shared himself with no other, he was the dragon's master. They say simply that having bound himself to a dragon, he must life-long keep faith with it. That love consumed him in the end."

What light there was left in the witch's voice fell splintered into Remus's dark hair.

"Remember the promise," she coughed, an autumnal gust through dry nettles. "Whisper thanks to me three times before each telling."

There was a rattle in her throat like dried beans spilled on stone. Her head fell against the back of the rocker and the only light in her gaping mouth was the glare of the rising sun.

Even as he slit her throat with the dagger drawn quietly from his boot, Remus knew she was dead. Steam hissed from the gashed neck, a sudden cloud of grey moths spilled out and dissolved in the air. Remus heard for the last time the ghost of her voice's beauty, "Remember my name, remember meee . . . " And then the frail words followed Mali into whatever darkness held her.

As Remus wiped the dust from his blade, the crone's body withered to the husk of a shed snake's skin.

"That's that," Remus said to himself.

He felt the story curled and powerful within himself, held his hands to his mouth, blew, and laughed as he saw phosphorescence splash into his palms.

Then the glass house began to crack. It seemed to wait for Remus to escape and then collapsed with a melancholy tinkling. The splintered pile blazed like a jagged, brittle rose bush and then softly fell to dust.

Funereal wails rose from the depths of the forest and blended into a ululating dirge. Remus felt the trees lour over him. The forest shifted its shadows to reclaim the witch's glade. With the sound of vellum pages turning in a grimoire, ravens flapped down and lit in the stark branches. They cocked their heads and watched Remus silently with their bright, black eyes. The wails grew louder, closer. Remus knew it was time to leave.

He pulled his cloak around him and threw himself down the path that led out of the forest. There was a crinkle of reflection. Without breaking stride, Remus saw that Mali had sewn his Guild Medallion back onto his cloak with golden thread. The Medallion was melted inextricably into the fabric. Remus didn't care. If it was the dead woman's fancy to remind him of his art, he was indifferent. Remus had what he had wanted, what he needed to transcend mere storytelling.

When he reached the edge of the forest, Remus looked back. Winged shapes drew to a pillar of luminous blue smoke; mournful, howling cries saturated the wind. But no eldritch forms flitted through the trees behind him, and Remus knew that the witch's final rites held no danger for him. He turned away from the forest and walked in the direction of the morning sun, for the weed-split stone of the Old Road, to retrace the journey of his quest and vault himself to the stage of his first triumph, the public telling of the story that he had found.

HERE WAS A HARSH RAP AT the door and Johan opened it narrowly, to keep the deluge from flooding the hallway.

"Let me enter, old man. It is I, Remus, your son."

Johan swung the door open, and the hooded figure strode into the house, seeming to bear the storm in with him. Johan caught the blaze of the Guild Medallion with its strange gold thread, and then Remus threw back the hood and looked around the small house with disinterested remembrance.

"My son, my child," Johan said with tearful concern, "the quest has made you a man."

He looked into Remus's drawn face.

"A man and more," said Remus, blowing on his hands.

Johan stared as the pulsating radiance in his son's breath outlined the bones of Remus's fingers.

"I can see that you have found more than a story, Remus," Johan said, aghast. "It's late and your mother sleeps. You can greet her in the morning. Rest now. Your room is as it was when you left." He led the gaunt stranger to his son's room and took his cloak. Remus stumbled in and fell on the narrow bed.

Light geysered from Remus's face as the weary, hypnotic voice commanded his father. "Display my cloak and Medallion in the Guild Hall tomorrow as proof that I have returned. Tell them that I am ready to face the public trial of my story." Remus' voice slurred and his father heard the soft cadence of sleep and saw the rhythmic flash of his son's breath in the dark bedroom.

Johan quietly closed the door, hung his son's cloak on the pegs in the hallway, wondered at the preternatural effulgence of his son's voice. He stood for a moment in the hall, staring at the Medallion that throbbed on the damp, stained cloth like a salamander in the heart of a furnace.

When Johan awoke the next morning, he told Rose that their son had returned and must not be disturbed. Then he walked to the Guild Hall as soon as it opened, hung the cloak with its golden Medallion on the door in display, and with an uneasy satisfaction, announced to Simon the Guildmaster that Remus had returned bearing a story and demanded public trial.

In secret Guild Council, the dice were thrown, the lots drawn, and the time of the telling of Remus's story chosen. Although the speaking platform was immediately erected in front of the Guild Hall, it was four days before Remus was summoned to try the mettle of the story he had found.

In Johan and Rose's house in Sparrow Alley, Remus waited hungrily in his shaded bedroom for the moment when he would unleash his story. He barely deigned to speak to his parents, asked them to leave him to prepare his spirit for the ordeal. They respected his wishes, took his inclination for nervous anticipation. They did not see that it was a profound and total scorn for the simple people who through some accident had honored themselves with his birth.

Throughout the city, the Guild itself spread rumors, suppositions, and expectations for Remus's public trial. While no one in the Guild had seen Remus or talked to him, these rumors served to guarantee a large audience for Remus and to publicize the Guild. It was late fall: the harvests had been brought in. Throughout the city, the adolescent, the jaded, and the curious gathered choice selections of fruit and deliquescent vegetables to pelt Remus with, should his story fail to hold interest. Such was the fickle temper of those times.

And so it was, that at the second hour of the night watch, on a cool and bracing autumn evening, the brass trumpets of the Guild of Seers, Speakers, Dreamers, Storytellers, and Non-Fanatical Prophets summoned the populace of Smunsk to judge the Quest-Tale of Remus.

Remus commanded that the torches in the square be extinguished, and the resinous, winy odor of their smoke swam through the night. Remus turned from the crowd and spoke softly to the vacancy between the rowels of the stars: ''Thanks to you, old witch, for the gift of story and the strength of speaking.'' Remus whispered Mali's name three times into the sere, chill wind and felt his thanks spin away to feed the darkness. Angry voices rose at this unexpected delay.

Remus pushed the hood of his cloak back, turned to the crowd, and blew a plume of dragonish fire out over the fractious faces which stilled the murmurs of impatience. He cast his mind out and felt the angry strength of the mob. Though there were too many for him to command,

51

like a skillful wrestler Remus used the impetuous rush of their anger to throw them into the Story of the Dragon. Since Mali's gift of eloquence, his mind-force had not increased, but had grown infinitely more delicate. Now when he rode the story as Kazan himself had ridden Almara, Remus realized that he had only to tell the Tale and the listeners themselves would toil like monks to illuminate its borders. He knew (and perhaps this was the lunar enchantment that Mali had chained to his breath) that the most binding seduction lay in this participation, where without thought, each listener sketched the faces of Fiona and Kazan with those they adored or scorned, filled the infinite details of scene and setting with their own lives.

As he chiseled the crowd with his fancies, Remus fed on the sobbing awe of their faces. When he was done, and the sucking, tidal adulation began to break on him, Remus staggered away in the darkness, dripping gobbets of light, stumbled home to his room in Sparrow Alley and barred the door to family and sudden friends. Weakness loosened his joints, and he faced the price that all who burn with a true story pay. Exhaustion rose from the bed and engulfed him.

The crowd in the square stood clotted with amazement, stood until their voices had gone hoarse and their hands swollen with applause. At last some of the less giddy Guild members relit the torches, and all the listeners weaved home, fuzzy with the lateness of the hour and the downslope of exhilaration.

The Guild of Seers, Speakers, Dreamers, Storytellers and Non-Fanatical Prophets held the Guild Admission Celebration posthaste. In Remus's absence, all toasted

Johan and Rose, and Guildmaster Simon, whose protege Remus had been acknowledged. After an hour of flagons and songs, no one missed Remus. Indeed, all were more comfortable in honoring his antecedents than in actually facing the possessor of such daunting talents.

None noticed the silence of Remus's parents, who sensed that while raising a Guild-Legend, they had also witnessed the transmutation of their son into something of more than mortal stature.

Mindless of the wind's increase and the churning approach of the first winter storm, a figure that had stood at the back of the crowd vaulted onto his horse and spurred its flanks. Casio, knight of the White Eagle Couriers, galloped down the wide road to the storied walls and stalwart gates of Datal, castle of King Cinnabar the Second. Casio knew that his rank was assured if he were the first to bear to Cinnabar's ear the word of the eruption of such a storyteller. The knight also knew that the King was chary of all those capable of stirring the populace. Cinnabar was well aware of the difference in regard between those who raised taxes and those who raised spirits. Down the hard, cold road Casio raced, with the news that secured Cinnabar's gratitude, and, as all the stories tell, the final fortune of Remus the Light-Spiller, Master of the Tale of the Dragon.

Two months passed before Cinnabar invited Remus to court. The King sent out spies to watch the storyteller and attend his performances. Ostensibly, it was to assure himself of the propriety of having Remus exhibit his skill.

But behind it all was the King's concern for a being whose word-power created so many instantaneous admirers. Meanwhile, as the word of his debut in Smunsk sizzled about the kingdom, Remus plotted with deliberate caution. He had already begun to receive offers from fairs, nobility, and certain religious orders, the acceptance of which would assure him mere wealth.

On the strength of his reputation (and some thought-twisting), Remus rented a beautiful estate outside of Smunsk and lived a life of such luxury as he felt would further his fame. He insulated himself from his parents and the Guild. The few times he appeared in public, Remus confirmed the noble and worthy arrogance expected of such a talent.

Remus finally accepted a commission from the Barbers, Bleeders, and Surgeons to provide the final entertainment at their annual convocation. Though it was a smaller audience than Remus might have commanded, his choice was a wise one. By the time the plump members of the audience had been washed with Remus's light and rose in a havoc of applause through the cunning cozening of his mind-bonds, Remus knew that his name would echo back to all the villages these healers served. And that each listener would celebrate Remus's tale-spinning to his patients. For the entertainments of healers are the thoughtless aspirations of the afflicted.

Remus's next appearance was for the assembled multitudes of the Fire-Fall Celebration. As the first meteors sang down in their lucent cat scratches, Remus stood on a high mound at the end of the Valley of Watchers and threw the flash and splendor of his voice out over the breath-hitched thousands who sat on the dark grass giving thanks for the falling stars. Throughout the lives of all who heard him that night, Remus's memory and the refraction of his words were bound forever to the heaven-sent wash of the Fire-Fall, that most joyful and beauteous of annual occasions, the divine shower of stars. Small matter that some were trampled in the rush of ecstatic pilgrims who surged up to touch this singer whose voice itself mirrored the prodigious sweep of the night's sidereal pageantry.

After this spectacle, a troop of cavalry rode up to Remus's estate and, with a swoop and flourish of plumes, gave the major-domo the tiny folded invitation sealed with Cinnabar's signet.

"Our Royal Master here signifies his pleasure and asks that the most illustrious Story-Wielder Remus perform for us a month hence."

From a high tower window, through a slit in the sable draperies, Remus saw the confirmation of his triumph, heard his servant's rehearsed reply.

"When my master ceases the mystic toils and communion with spirits that are daily necessary for the maintenance of his gifts, I will present him with this token of his signal honor."

The courtier bowed from his horse and gestured at the bullion wagon lumbering up to Remus's door.

"The benevolent and generous Cinnabar offers this small token of his artistic appreciation," the knight said, drawing the canvas cover from the wagon's bed.

The mound of gold coins glowed like a dragon's hoard.

Remus watched from his window as the King's emissaries clattered down the cobbled road. The heaped dower of his story-prowess glistened like the sun's blood.

He stared at this reflection of his heart's fire, smiled, and began to make his plans.

The palomino had almost pranced by the two drab figures before Remus recognized his parents. They stood under the trees that overhung the curling ironwork of the gates to Remus's estate. The coaches of the mummers, the minstrels singing on their sturdy ponies, the ox-drawn carts with their oiled canvas shielding the folding scenery; all these had contributed to the dust that clung to Johan and Rose.

"We heard of your royal commission and came to see you off," Johan said.

His parents stood together and looked up at Remus with affection that turned his stomach. Their son knew that they might not have spoken if he had not seen them and stopped. His horse danced impatiently.

"I am off to make my fortune," Remus told them, looking into the humid air, off toward the High Court of Datal. "I will return and raise you two from the squalor of Sparrow Alley."

"Spare those who love you false promises," Rose told him. "You leave and would forget us."

"Dear mother, I pass from a feeble and benighted profession to the pantheon. I am beyond mere stories. I am past words. I am the voice made light. I . . . "

" . . . have forgotten that the speaker is not greater than his story or the story greater than its teller. That we speak to move and not to control." Against his wishes, Johan had risen to anger.

"My weak-skilled father," Remus replied, his voice corroded with pity, "as I ascend from your narrow world, remember how I have dwarfed the stunted, carping tenets of your beloved Guild."

Remus drew a weighty purse from his brocaded jacket, threw it at his parents' feet with contemptuous largesse. He whipped his horse once and cantered away.

"Blasphemer," the old man spoke, choking on his spittle. He picked up the purse and threw it with feeble violence at the vanishing horseman.

"Sweet fool," Rose told him and walked to retrieve the gold.

Remus led his caravan slowly down the long road to Datal. His ponderous retinue prevented speed. And Remus knew that it was better to let word of his coming precede him. They camped outside towns, never stayed at inns, knowing that mysteries gave greater aura than the taint of facts.

When they did proceed through villages and small cities on the way to Datal, it was at mid-day, so they could clog traffic and the curious hordes could marvel at the numbers of Remus's host, at the massive black wagons carved with fearsome imps and crawling symbols of a nameless zodiac. Within his own great coach fashioned like a dragon with folded wings, Remus fed on the whispered speculation and superstitious fear. As they dragged the monstrous coach with its lapis lazuli scales, the albino dromedaries spat with ungainly malevolence on all who came close.

The very animals added to the imperious air of Remus's nobility with their random, violent tempers.

When he received the royal invitation, Remus had gathered to him the itinerant painters, mummers, actors, musicians, and minstrels, of whom there were the usual hungry superfluity. At his command, they had begun the majestic labors which Remus deemed necessary to stage the Tale of the Dragon before Cinnabar, his court and the populace of the royal city of Datal. For while Remus had absolute confidence in the naked power of his telling of the Story, he was succumbing to a self-importance that demanded embellishment. With his hirelings, the artisans of art, and the physical trappings of spectacle, Remus was trying to provide a gaudy frame for the vitality of his beaming speech and the stern enchantment of his story.

The witch had faded to a distant, insubstantial memory. More and more, Remus believed that the story was his and that by tricking it out in this impressive artificiality, he had tamed it. Soon, with the subtle powers of his mind-force and the hypnotic fire of his voice, Remus would move to subjugate Datal and then the remaining Five Kingdoms and the wide world beyond. And perhaps later, he could speak the sun to rise and fall.

The woesome dragon's head on Remus's coach bobbed up and down and the brazier of charcoal cast refracted flames through its garnet eyes as the sentry called to the caravan from the high walls of Datal: ''Who would enter the fortress of Datal, seat and treasure of mighty Cinnabar the Second?''

From the belly of his dragon coach, Remus heard his page's reply: "We come at Royal Command to perform for his Majesty. We are Remus, Lord of Light and Master of the Tale of the Dragon, and the performers and possessions of his company."

"You are awaited and expected by our most interested King. We will lead you to your quarters in the palace."

At the captain's order, the grim brass gates swung open and Remus and his procession made their torchlit way to the opulent chambers of the East Wing of the palace. Even at this late hour, clumps of citizens stood and gawked at the passage of the fabled speaker and his fantastical equipage. Remus made a quick mind-cast. Datal was ripe with his rumor and reputation. Even the dreams of the sleeping city were tinged with his name.

"We are well pleased. Pleased and greater than pleased." Cinnabar held out his hand for Remus to kiss.

Remus lightly brushed the King's knuckles with his lips, avoiding the beetle-backed ring that held a cache of poison. "Your thanks is my greatest reward," Remus answered traditionally.

The King's family stared slack-mouthed at the storyteller. Though Remus had reined his powers in for this private presentation of the tale in the royal chambers, the low flicker of his speaking had rendered all in the small room speechless.

"Nevertheless," the king said, "I can tell from my daughter's eyes that I will have no peace until you are fitly rewarded."

The fair girl blushed in her gilt chair as her father laughed. Then from behind his long silver beard, Cinnabar drew forth a leather pouch and handed it to Remus.

"A token," the King apologized.

From mind-theft of Cinnabar, Remus knew the pouch contained a plum-sized ruby of the first water. "My most unworthy thanks," Remus replied.

"Our appreciation again for this private performance, Story-Lord. I know the anxious details of preparation you still must attend to for the public performance before all our subjects."

Remus took the cue and bowed to them again. "Your leave," he said, "to provide for the entertainment of your loving subjects."

"As you depart," Cinnabar smiled gently, "let us walk with you and exchange a few pleasantries."

With silent humility, Remus followed the King to the archway at the far end of the chamber.

"If you charm our assembled subjects in your public performance tomorrow night with the same majesty you brought to this private display, we will find a place for you at Court," the king promised, blandly stroking his beard.

Seemingly tongue-tied with joy, Remus nodded his gratitude. He had read the King's mind all evening, knew that assassins lurked behind the arras, knew that if the city of Datal was as moved as the King's family had been, the King would put him in the damp, sweat-stone depths of his stronghold and he would end his life strangled with a greased bowstring.

"I wish you could read the joy in my heart," Remus told the King.

The rivet-studded door swung to let Remus pass, and

the King again gave Remus the benison of his smile.

Without thinking, Remus whistled the Guild Song of the Stalker as he made his way back to his troop. Tomorrow night he would make the crowd worship him, then blast the King with a spasm of light as he sat in his royal box. The guards would side with Remus, with some thought coercion and slight gold. Then he would marry the Princess and rule the kingdom that would be the foundation of his conquests.

Later Remus puffed wreaths of light into the dim corners of his chambers as he oversaw the painting, sawing, and hammering of his minions. Tomorrow night, he would allow the King to crown him Lord of Datal, Ruler of the First Kingdom.

The crowd gathered in the great square of Datal, a host worthy of a coronation or a royal funeral. Its size was not lost on Cinnabar, nor the perfunctory interest they displayed for one of his rare public appearances. If the storyteller lived up to his promise, it would be death for the radiance-spilling sorcerer.

Cinnabar looked on his daughter with barely controlled disgust as she joined the chants of "REEEMUUUSS, REEEMUUUS" that rolled back and forth across the square.

Finally, as night settled on Datal like a raven's belly, minstrels stepped from the shadows of the stage and soothed the crowd with recorders, finger drums and the uncanny drone of bagpipes. Smudge pots were lit by unseen hands and smoke rolled in slow thunderheads over the audience. Mummers rose and fell, capered and sprang across the boards in eerie pantomime of souls who had lost the darkling path to salvation. And in a moment of hesitation and frozen gesture, the ropes and silent pulleys of the scene painters spread the huge dragon wings of canvas that had been folded at the sides of the stage. At staggering expense, the wings had been edged with the star-silver of the last elven chromatic dreamers, and as the starlight hit the blessed tinctures, the scales of the false dragon's wings burned with lunar, sympathetic brilliance.

In this hiatus of breath and thought, Remus stepped forward into the wavering glare of the smudge pots at the edge of the stage. He raised his arms and the false, glittering scales of elvish paint shone against the black goatskin of his costume. The crowd teetered on the brink of worship, and Remus felt Cinnabar's serpentine thoughts pronounce his doom. Remus tasted the diapason of brilliance welling within his throat and knew that after he had seduced the crowd with The Tale of the Dragon, Cinnabar himself would fall from power.

With his trappings, his hirelings, the orchestration of this stupefying stagecraft that forged these listeners to such malleable anticipation, Remus knew that he had finally gained control of the story that he had received months before in the glass cottage from the dying witch's lips.

So it was that Remus, in his overweening joy, did not thank Mali three times for the boon of the story.

"Once upon a time," Remus began and saw the spellbinding radiance break over the crowd and rush to the far walls of the royal square, splash, and return in a luminous seiche. Never had he such woesome power, never had the light raced in such a cataclysmic torrent.

He held the crowd in such sway that they did not hear what drew near, until the end. Remus was taken with himself, savoring his word-mastery, the reflections and refractions he gave his glistening voice, slavering at the submission of so many hearts. So taken that he did not notice how a single great cloud sped over the night, blotted constellations dark for a moment and drew swiftly closer.

Remus looked up when he felt the buffet of wind, heard the deep, almost apologetic cough from the living darkness above him. It was not until then that his control faltered, that the light broke, and the whole crush of upturned faces saw in terror what Remus saw and not what he willed.

In huge concussive gusts, the dragon lowered herself into the glare of the smudge pots and hovered above the storyteller. No sophistry of elvish paint, stagecraft, or fable could approach the glittering, molten presence of the flying worm. And though none such beast had been seen in over four centuries, the crowd's recognition was as instinctive as its fear.

The dragon bent her head down from the darkness and if such a creature can be said to smile, she smiled. The smudge pots and torches around Remus paled in the seething glare of her one huge eye, and their weak fire played on the corded golden cables that bound shut the hollow socket of her other eye.

For one crisp moment, man and dragon shared recognition. Then with a grievous, grieving bellow, the dragon incinerated Remus, the stage, the royal box, and the immediate listeners with the virulent sear of a comet's tale.

So many in Datal had come to hear Remus that even the voracious appetite of the dragon was slaked. Some few remained cowering in basements and cisterns to flesh the deeds of the night to story. Finally the abomination threw herself into the depths of the firmament and flew with black, sure strokes back to her lair in the high cold peaks of the Dolorous Mountains, from where, centuries before, Kazan the Thief had borne her to the world and ways of men.

In the narrow house in Sparrow Alley, Rose and Johan looked up from their supper and sat with twisted mouths as the stacked coins their son had thrown them smoked and fell to cinders in the table's center.

"Our son has died," Rose stated.

"His body followed his heart," Johan amended.

They daubed their eyes as they stared at the fire's ruin.

"He finally broke faith with his story," the father wept.

"Perhaps he betrayed love," Rose hoped quietly.

For as usual in marriages, they spoke the same thought in different words.

Photo by Joseph Schuyler

Michael Rutherford is the author of a poetry chapbook, **Meat Is My Business**, and the translator of **Lesbia-Catullus**. He is the founder and director of Alternative Literary Programs in the Schools (ALPS), which sponsors workshops and readings by local writers in New York State, and he is a winner of the Albany League of the Arts Annual Award for Artistic Excellence.

112   22

This book was printed and bound by Coneco Laser Graphics at Glens Falls in New York. The type is Palacio and the paper is acid-free.